August Acrobat

A figure appeared from the back of the tent and climbed one of the poles. Whoever it was wore silver tights that shimmered under the lights. A silver hood covered the figure's head and eyes. Only the nose and mouth could be seen.

At the top of the pole, the silver person unhooked a trapeze swing that had been tied to the pole. With a leap, the figure was sitting on the trapeze bar. Then he or she stood and began swinging back and forth.

Down below, the kids stood with their mouths open, watching.

Bradley could hardly swallow. Even with the net under the trapeze, it would be a long way to fall.

August Acrobat

by **Ron Roy**

illustrated by
John Steven Gurney

A STEPPING STONE BOOK™

Random House 🏠 New York

*This book is dedicated to parents
who read to and with their children.*
—R.R.

To Mark, Julia, and Maxi
—J.S.G.

Text copyright © 2012 by Ron Roy
Cover art, map, and interior illustrations copyright © 2012 by John Steven Gurney

Visit us on the Web!
ronroy.com
randomhouse.com/kids

Educators and librarians, for a variety of teaching tools,
visit us at randomhouse.com/teachers

Library of Congress Cataloging-in-Publication Data
Roy, Ron.
August acrobat / by Ron Roy ; illustrated by John Steven Gurney.
  p. cm. — (Calendar mysteries)
"A Stepping Stone Book."
Summary: Bradley, Brian, Nate, and Lucy try to help out the Flying Fortunatos, an acrobatic troupe with a very shabby traveling circus, by identifying the marvelous, hooded trapeze artist they spied rehearsing.
ISBN 978-0-375-86886-3 (trade) — ISBN 978-0-375-96886-0 (lib. bdg.) — ISBN 978-0-375-89969-0 (ebook)
[1. Mystery and detective stories. 2. Acrobats—Fiction. 3. Circus—Fiction. 4. Twins—Fiction. 5. Brothers and sisters—Fiction. 6. Cousins—Fiction.] I. Gurney, John Steven, ill. II. Title.
PZ7.R8139Aug 2012 [Fic]—dc23 2011037689

Printed in the United States of America

10 9 8 7 6 5 4 3 2 1

Contents

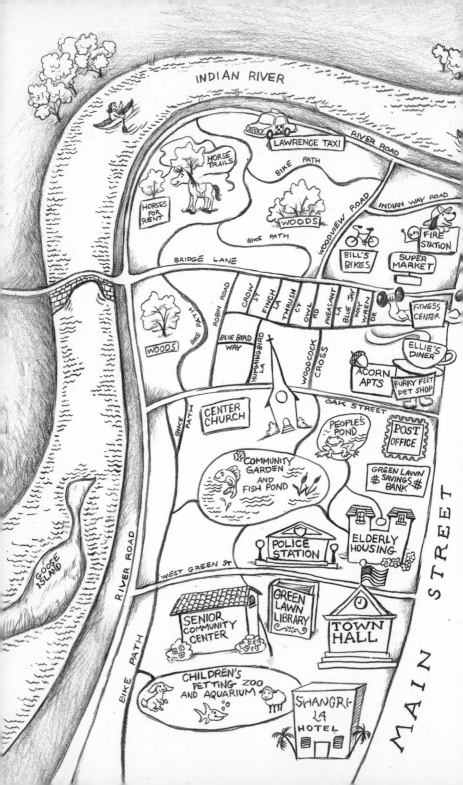

1
The Flying Fortunatos

Bradley Pinto pushed open the door of the Shangri-la Hotel. Inside, the lobby was quiet and cool. Comfortable furniture was placed around a big red carpet. A ceiling fan hummed, blowing air through the room.

Behind the hotel counter stood Mr. Linkletter. He calmly watched as Bradley walked toward him.

"Hi, Mr. Linkletter," Bradley said. He flashed his best smile.

Everyone in Green Lawn liked Mr.

Linkletter, even though he almost never smiled. His mustache did wrinkle a little now and then, however.

Bradley noticed that the mustache was wrinkling now. That was almost a smile!

"Good morning, young Mr. Pinto," Mr. Linkletter said. "Are you Bradley or Brian?"

"I'm Bradley," Bradley said.

"How does your family tell you two apart?"

Bradley grinned. "Our freckles are different," he said.

Mr. Linkletter blinked once, then nodded. He shoved the hotel register book in front of Bradley. "Checking in?" he asked. "How long will you be staying?"

Bradley laughed. "You're joking with me, right?"

"I never joke," Mr. Linkletter said.

But the mustache moved upward, and his kind eyes gleamed. "Why *are* you here, Mr. Bradley?"

Bradley pulled a pile of tickets from his pocket. They were held together with a rubber band. He removed one ticket and showed it to Mr. Linkletter. "Would you like to buy a ticket?" he asked. "They're two dollars each."

Mr. Linkletter took the ticket and read what was printed on the blue paper. "Who are the Flying Fortunatos?" he asked.

"It's like a circus," Bradley explained. "They're acrobats . . . I think. Anyway, they're coming to town Monday. Brian, Nate, Lucy, and I are selling tickets!"

Mr. Linkletter's eyebrows moved up toward his hair, like two jumping caterpillars. "Why?" he asked Bradley.

"Why what?" Bradley asked right back.

"Why are you selling tickets for the Flying Fortunatos?"

"Oh. See, Brian read in one of his comics that the circus was looking for kids to sell tickets, so he signed us up for one hundred," Bradley explained.

He held up his stack. "We each have to sell twenty-five," he added. "If we sell them all, we get in free! Plus we get free popcorn and hot dogs. I really like hot dogs!"

Mr. Linkletter gazed down at Bradley for a moment. Finally, the mustache twitched. "I'll take four," Mr. Linkletter said, reaching for his wallet. "My three nephews will be my guests."

"Awesome, thank you!" Bradley shouted. He pulled three more tickets out and slid them toward Mr. Linkletter.

Mr. Linkletter handed Bradley eight crisp dollar bills. "You're very welcome," he said, slipping the tickets into his suit jacket pocket. "Where will you go next?"

Bradley glanced out the window. "The town hall, I guess," he said. "I have this whole section of town."

"The town hall is closed on Saturday," Mr. Linkletter said. He leaned over the counter. "Try the senior center. I have a feeling those folks would like to see flying acrobats." His mustache wrinkled. "And they really like hot dogs, too."

"Thanks again, Mr. Linkletter," Bradley said. He took his twenty-one tickets and flew out the door.

2
The Strange Note

Bradley sold the rest of his tickets at the senior center. His friend Mr. Neater lived there, and he introduced Bradley to each guest. Almost everyone said, "I haven't seen a circus in years!" And just like that, Bradley's pockets were stuffed with dollar bills.

He was the first one home, too. He found a note on the kitchen table.

Hi, boys. Dad's running errands.
I've taken Josh to buy new sneakers.

Be back in a jiffy.
Love,
Mom

Bradley smiled. He liked the word *jiffy*. He ran upstairs, almost stumbling over Pal, who was sleeping outside Bradley's bedroom door.

In his room, Bradley dropped fifty crumpled dollar bills all over his neatly made bed.

That's a lot of money! Bradley told himself. *I'd better hide it.* Bradley's brother Josh had told him about the burglar in Green Lawn a few years ago. Josh and his friends Ruth Rose and Dink had helped catch him.

Ruth Rose was Nate's big sister, and Dink was Lucy's cousin.

Bradley knew he shouldn't hide the money in his piggy bank. That was the first place a burglar would look!

Then he spied the empty shoe box that the one hundred tickets had come in. *It's perfect for all these dollar bills,* he thought. He grabbed the box off Brian's bed.

When Bradley took the lid off, he saw a crumpled paper on the bottom. He took the paper out and put his money into the box.

Flopping on his bed, Bradley smoothed out the paper. He smiled. It was a drawing of a circus elephant standing on its hind legs. Monkeys were hanging on the elephant's ears, trunk, and tail. A parrot sat on top of the elephant's head.

In the four corners of the picture were small drawings of acrobats. They were swinging, tumbling, and walking on high wires. Two of the acrobats were older people, a man and a woman with white hair. There were two drawings of a third acrobat, a younger one with short, dark hair.

Bradley noticed small rips in the paper, near the elephant's hind legs. He turned the picture over. On the back, someone had written a note in pencil. Bradley read it:

Dear Mr. Wood,
I hope you like this picture.
Can you help me?
I hate being an acrobat!!!
I want to

Bradley couldn't read the rest of the note. The words had been blackened out by dark pencil scribbles. Whoever did the scribbling must have been pushing the pencil down hard. In places, it had poked through the paper.

I wonder who wrote this note, Bradley thought. *And who's Mr. Wood?*

And who scribbled out those final words?

Bradley crossed the room and tacked the picture to his bulletin board.

Pal shuffled into the room and put his paws up on Bradley's bed. He sniffed the shoe box.

"Where should I hide this money?" Bradley asked Pal.

Pal flopped down on the floor and closed his eyes.

"You're no help," Bradley muttered, looking around his room. Maybe in the closet? He stepped inside just as the bedroom door swung open. Brian burst into the room, chased by Lucy and Nate.

"I'm first!" Brian cried.

"You cheated!" Nate yelled.

"Did not. You're just slow," Brian retorted. "I'm fast and I'm first!"

Bradley stepped out of the closet. "No, bro. You're slow and you're second," he announced. *"I'm* fast and I'm first!"

"What're you doing here?" Brian demanded. "You're supposed to be selling tickets."

"Sold them all," Bradley said. He opened the shoe box and showed them the stack of dollar bills.

"No way!" Brian yelled.

"Yes way," Bradley said.

He dropped the box of money on his bed. "How'd you guys do?"

"I sold all mine!" Lucy said. She pulled a wad of bills out of her shorts pocket. "The people in Green Lawn sure are nice!"

"Me too," Nate said. "When I got to Howard's Barbershop, a bunch of guys were waiting to get their hair cut. Everyone wanted tickets. I could have sold a million more!"

The three kids turned and looked

at Brian. "I still have two left," he said. "Plus the three I'm selling to Josh, Mom, and Dad."

"That's okay," Bradley said. "We can sell those other two in a *jiffy*. You guys want to stick your money in this box with mine?"

Brian, Nate, and Lucy added their money to Bradley's fifty dollars.

"Wow, that's a lot of money," Brian whispered. "Almost . . ."

"It's exactly one hundred and ninety dollars," Lucy said.

"Right," Brian said. "I was just going to say that."

Bradley shoved the box under his bed. "The Green Lawn burglar will never look there!" he said.

"Who's the Green Lawn burglar?" Lucy asked.

The three boys began telling her what happened the last time a circus came to Green Lawn.

3
The Mystery Acrobat

Brian sold the rest of his tickets the next day. Josh and his parents each gave him two dollars, and he sold the last two tickets to Ellie when the kids were having ice cream at her diner.

Brian added his ten dollars to the money in the box, then slid it back under Bradley's bed. Now the box held two hundred dollars.

"When do we have to give the money to the acrobats?" Lucy asked.

"I don't know," Bradley said. He

looked at his calendar. "Um, Bri, when does the circus open?"

"Tomorrow. Why? Oh my gosh!" Brian said. "They're supposed to set up their tent tonight! Maybe they're already here!"

"All right," Nate said, rubbing his stomach. "Let's bring them the money and get our free popcorn and hot dogs!"

"I don't want to walk around town carrying all that money," Bradley said. "Let's just go see if the Flying Fortunatos are here yet. We can give them the money later."

The others agreed, and they took off toward the high school, where the circus was going to be. When they passed Nate's house on Woody Street, they waved to his sister. She was in the backyard with Dink and Josh. They cut across Pleasant Street and headed toward the high school playing fields.

When they came out of the trees, they stopped.

A hundred feet in front of them stood a giant tent. The tent leaned to one side, as if it wanted to go to sleep. A canvas flap was tied open. It was dim inside, but Bradley could see seats and some kind of pole with wires on it.

Across the lawn from the tent, they saw a long trailer with a door and four small windows. Narrow steps were

under the door. The words THE FLYING FORTUNATOS were painted under the row of windows. The paint was so faded that they could hardly read it.

Parked near the trailer was an old Volkswagen bus that needed to be washed.

The kids didn't see any elephants or tigers.

Or men being shot out of cannons.

Or any Flying Fortunatos.

Bradley felt his stomach drop like a water balloon. *We sold a hundred tickets for this?* he thought.

"It's a pretty small circus," Lucy said.

"It's not a circus," Bradley said. "It's a disaster!"

"At least they have a tent," Nate said. "Let's look inside."

The kids walked around the tent to the open flap. They stepped inside and looked around. Without the sunlight, it was dark. They saw tall poles with a net stretched between them. They heard soft music, the kind that made you dream about faraway places.

"There's nobody—" Nate started to say.

Suddenly bright lights lit up the space.

A figure appeared from the back of the tent and climbed one of the poles. Whoever it was wore silver tights that shimmered under the lights. A silver hood covered the figure's head and eyes. Only the nose and mouth could be seen.

At the top of the pole, the silver person unhooked a trapeze swing that had been tied to the pole. With a leap, the figure was sitting on the trapeze bar. Then he or she stood and began swinging back and forth.

Down below, the kids stood with their mouths open, watching.

Bradley could hardly swallow. Even with the net under the trapeze, it would be a long way to fall.

But the figure in silver tights didn't fall. He or she swung, turned flips, and did a hundred other tricks on the trapeze.

"That's amazing!" Nate whispered. "He's like Spider-Man!"

"How do you know it's a man?" Lucy asked. She gazed up at the trapeze artist.

"Sorry, you're right, Lucy," Nate said. "It could be a girl."

"She's like a silver waterfall," Lucy said. "Wouldn't you love to be able to do that?"

"I don't know," Brian said. "It gives my stomach goose bumps just watching!"

Suddenly the figure was off the trapeze and down the pole. Without even glancing toward the kids, the acrobat dashed toward the back of the tent. The lights went off, and the kids were standing in the dark again.

4
The Lousy Acrobat

The kids stepped out of the tent and sat under a big maple tree. They looked at the trailer and old bus. The only things moving were the leaves on the tree.

"Shouldn't there be clowns running around?" Nate asked. "Shouldn't there be—"

Just then the trailer door opened. A man came out, carrying a folding table. He had white hair and a round belly. He set up the table under a tree near the trailer.

Then he went back and held the

door open. A teenage boy wearing gym shorts and a T-shirt stepped down. He was lugging some lawn chairs, which he placed around the table. Behind him, a woman with gray hair came out with a tray of food.

"You think those are the Flying Fortunatos?" Nate whispered.

Brian giggled.

Bradley remembered the picture he'd found in the shoe box. In the corners, there had been little drawings of acrobats doing stunts. Were these the same people?

"Should we go meet them?" Lucy asked.

"No!" Brian said. "Let's watch them a little. I want to make sure this circus is for real before they ask us for that money!"

The couple sat down. The man said something to the boy, but he shook his head. The door of the old bus opened, and a teenage girl came out. Her spiky, dark hair made her look as if she'd just gotten out of bed. She ran over to the others and sat down. The boy turned and marched away.

"He's headed for the tent," Nate said.

The boy had his head down. He seemed to be talking to himself, and he didn't look happy. And he never noticed the kids sitting under the tree. They watched the boy stomp through the open flap and disappear inside the tent.

"Now what?" Nate asked. "This is very weird."

A few seconds later, the boy appeared back outside the tent. He looked around, as if he thought someone was spying on him. Then he unhitched a cord on the tent, stepped inside, and tugged the flap over the opening.

"That kid looked kind of sneaky," Bradley said. "Like he didn't want anyone to see him."

"I like sneaky!" Nate said. "Let's go see what he's doing."

"Yeah," Brian agreed. The kids moved toward the tent.

"I don't know," Lucy said. "It feels like we're doing something wrong."

"We sold their tickets, remember?" Brian said. "We need to know what's going on around here."

They crouched down and scurried toward the closed flap. Bradley felt as if he was in a spy movie. He glanced over his shoulder toward the trailer. He couldn't see the Fortunatos—if that was who they were—so he figured they couldn't see him.

Bradley knelt where the flap closed, and raised the canvas until he could see inside. The lights came on, making Bradley jump backward.

Brian, Nate, and Lucy wriggled around Bradley so they could see through the tent flap.

This time Bradley noticed two big cages. One of them had a sign that said DANGER—FEROCIOUS LION.

The other one was longer and flatter than the lion cage. Its sign said ANNIE— THE WORLD'S LONGEST ANACONDA.

"There's a lion in there?" Nate squeaked in Bradley's ear.

"Why isn't it roaring or something?" Brian asked in Bradley's other ear.

Just then the teenage boy stepped out from behind the lion cage. He shinnied

up one of the poles, and before Bradley could even blink, the kid was walking across the high wire.

. Bradley thought the kid looked scared up there. The boy took a step, then began waving his arms. He lost his balance and fell into the net.

Then he went to a mat and started doing backflips. At least he *tried* to do backflips, but he kept falling onto the mat.

Next he went to the trapeze rings

and pulled himself up. But his legs were kicking and he couldn't do a single stunt. He dropped from the rings and stood there with a sad look on his face. He bent over, picked up a fistful of sawdust, and threw it at the rings. Then he ran for the exit. Straight toward the four kids!

They jumped away from the flap, but the boy didn't notice them as he bolted out of the tent.

Bradley saw the boy's face clearly as he dashed past. The teenager's mouth was set in a grimace, and tears were streaming down his cheeks.

5
Four Little Spies

The kids watched the boy run to the old bus. He yanked open the door, jumped inside, and slammed the door behind him.

"What's going on?" Nate asked. "He looks mad at somebody."

"He was crying," Bradley said.

"Yeah, because he's a lousy acrobat," Brian said. "That other one in the silver costume was awesome!"

"Maybe the kid is just jealous," Nate suggested.

"FOUR LITTLE SPIES!" a deep voice growled from behind the kids. "Maude, let's throw them in the lion's cage!"

The four kids jumped like kangaroos!

"No, Basilio, let's feed them to the snake," a woman's voice said. "Our anaconda hasn't eaten a child in weeks!"

Bradley nearly swallowed his tongue. Brian, Nate, and Lucy froze and stared at the man and woman.

"We . . . we . . . we . . ." Bradley couldn't make his mouth say anything.

"Well, speak up," the man barked. "Lion or snake? Your choice."

"I have a better idea, Papa," another voice said. It was the girl. She appeared from behind the woman.

"Do you guys like cookies?" the teenager asked the kids. She was smiling, and her hair was neatly brushed into place.

"We . . . love cookies!" Nate said, finally finding his voice.

"Oh heck, Maude," the man said to his wife. "I never get to have any fun."

Then he grinned at the kids. "Just teasing," he said. "Since Hannah won't let me feed you to the wild animals, we might as well feed you some of Mama Maude's outstanding cookies. Come along!"

The couple turned and walked toward the trailer. They were laughing as they strolled away, arm in arm.

"I'm Hannah Fortunato," the girl said, shaking the kids' hands. "Don't mind my folks. They love joking around. Most of the time they act younger than Adam and me."

The kids and Hannah headed toward the table, where her parents were waiting.

"Is Adam your brother?" Lucy asked. "We were watching him inside the tent."

"He's good," Hannah said.

Good? Bradley thought. *He's terrible!*

"My parents taught him," Hannah said. "They were the best once."

Bradley remembered the picture he'd hung on his bulletin board. "Do you do acrobatics, too?" he asked Hannah.

"Me? Oh, no," she said. "My job is mostly in the office, taking care of ticket sales and other stuff."

When they reached the table, Hannah's father stood up. He reached out a hand the size of a catcher's mitt. "I am Basilio Fortunato," he boomed. "And who are you?"

The kids all shook Basilio Fortunato's big hand.

"We're Brian and Bradley Pinto," Brian piped up. "We sold tickets for you!"

"Are you twins?" Maude asked the boys.

"Yep," Brian said. "I'm two minutes older than Bradley!"

"Hannah and Adam are twins, too," Maude said.

"And I'm Nate Hathaway, and this is Lucy Armstrong," Nate added. "We sold tickets, too!"

"Wonderful!" Maude said. "Sit and have cookies. They have nuts. Are you allergic?"

The kids all shook their heads and reached for the plate of cookies. They sat on the grass as Hannah poured glasses of lemonade.

"Do you really have a lion and an anaconda?" Nate asked.

Basilio sighed and rubbed his forehead. "We used to," he said. "And a horse named Roger. We had a real circus a few years ago, but now—"

"Now we have Adam, our son, who is the world's greatest acrobat," Maude interrupted.

Bradley thought about Adam in the

tent a few minutes ago. If he was their acrobat, this circus was worse off than he'd thought! Adam couldn't be the amazing acrobat in the silver costume!

"You guys talking about me?" a new voice asked.

Adam Fortunato joined the group. His hair was combed and he wore a fresh T-shirt. "Hope you left me some cookies, Mom."

Bradley looked at Adam. He seemed happy as he gobbled half a cookie in one gulp.

Then why was he crying ten minutes ago?

"What happened to the lion and anaconda?" Brian said. "We saw the cages in the tent."

"Had to sell 'em," Basilio muttered.

"You were in the tent?" Adam asked. His smile disappeared. Red spots appeared on his cheeks.

"We, um, sort of peeked," Bradley said.

"We didn't mean to be sneaky," Lucy said.

Adam looked as if he'd just swallowed a bug.

"Lighten up, Adam," Hannah said. "These kids sold a whole bunch of tickets for us."

"Great," Adam said. He lurched away toward the old bus.

Hannah looked at the kids. "Don't mind Adam," she said. "He's just not . . ." Then she shook her head and smiled at the kids. "So did you sell all one hundred?"

"Yep!" Nate said. "It was a snap. We could have sold more!"

"Super," Hannah said. "Can you come back after dinner tonight? We're going to have a quick rehearsal before we open tomorrow."

"Sure, we can come," Brian said.

"Come around seven, okay?" Hannah said. "You can see Adam perform, and Peter, too."

"Who's Peter?" Bradley asked.

"Peter is our parrot," Hannah's father said proudly. "He talks, he dances, he does tricks!"

"Peter is very cute," Maude said. "And we have Clumsy, the world's funniest clown!"

"I love clowns!" Lucy said.

Maude gave Hannah a hug. "We love her, too," she said. "Hannah is a wonderful clown!"

"Who else is in your show?" Bradley asked, thinking of the silver acrobat.

"No one else," said Hannah.

"Now we must excuse ourselves," Basilio said. "See you at seven."

The couple walked toward the tent.

"See you kids later," Hannah said as she headed toward the bus.

The kids started walking away from the high school grounds.

"Boy, we messed up," Brian said. "This isn't a circus at all!"

"Yeah, and we sold all those tickets," Nate said. "Everyone in town is going to be mad at us."

"Maybe we can help them," Lucy said.

"They need a lot more than our help," Bradley said. "All they have is a parrot and Hannah pretending to be a clown. How can they call themselves the Flying Fortunatos when they don't even have an acrobat? Adam is lousy!"

"But the person in the silver costume wasn't lousy!" Lucy said.

"So why didn't anyone mention that acrobat? Who was it?" Brian asked.

"Maybe it was Adam," Nate said.

"Dude, we saw Adam, and he stinks as an acrobat," Brian said.

Nate giggled. "Maybe it was Peter the parrot!"

Everyone just looked at Nate.

"I wonder where the silver acrobat went," Bradley said.

"And what was he doing in the Fortunatos' tent if he isn't a Fortunato?" Brian said.

"We can help the Fortunatos if we can find that acrobat!" Lucy said.

"But we don't know who it is," Nate said. "He just disappeared out the back of the tent. And most of his face was covered."

"People can't disappear," Lucy said. "We have to find the mystery acrobat by tomorrow!"

6
The Hairy Clue

"How are we going to find him?" Brian asked. "He could be anywhere!"

"I have one idea." Lucy turned and pointed at the tent. "The silver acrobat left through the back of the tent, right?"

"Right," Bradley said.

Lucy turned again and pointed toward Main Street. "So maybe he went to town," she added.

"Yeah!" Bradley said. "We can ask if anyone saw him."

"So we're supposed to just ask

everyone if they've seen some dude in silver tights?" Brian asked with a big grin.

"Why not?" asked Bradley.

"Yeah, why not?" repeated Nate.

"We have to try," Lucy said. "He or she could save the circus!"

"Ha!" Brian said.

"Lucy is right," Bradley said. "Where should we start?"

They cut through Center Park and walked past Swan Pond. Two minutes later they were on Main Street.

"Where would you go if you were an acrobat in silver tights?" Lucy asked.

"I'd go home and change," Nate said.

"I'd go to the fitness center and hide," Brian said.

Bradley laughed. "I'd go to Ellie's Diner for ice cream!" he said.

"Me too," Lucy said. The kids headed for Ellie's and crowded through the glass door.

Ellie was making banana splits for four teenagers sitting in a booth.

Bradley, Brian, and Nate sat at the counter and watched Ellie squirt whipped cream on top of the sundaes.

Lucy marched up to the booth. "Have you guys seen someone in silver tights?" she asked the four teenagers.

"Boy or girl?" one of the boys asked Lucy.

"We don't know," Lucy said.

The teenagers looked at each other. "Nope, we haven't seen anyone in tights since we saw the Spider-Man movie!"

Lucy joined the boys at the counter.

"I haven't, either," Ellie said. "Who is it?"

"That's what we're trying to find out," Bradley said. He and the other kids explained about the circus and the masked acrobat.

"Wow," said Ellie. "I hope you find him or her. And if they need help tomorrow, let me know. I have a popcorn maker in my basement!"

The kids thanked Ellie and headed next door to the fitness center.

Bradley stopped at the desk. "Excuse me," he said to the man working there. "We're looking for someone in silver tights who might have come in a little while ago."

"Did you look in the gym?" the man asked. "Lots of people wearing tights in there." He pointed to a large window.

Inside the gym, the kids saw people lifting weights, doing stretches, and walking on treadmills. Some of them wore workout tights. A couple of the outfits were silver. But none looked like the costume the acrobat was wearing.

The kids left the fitness center and walked down Main Street. They asked Mrs. Wong in the pet shop.

They stopped in the bookstore.

They questioned an attendant at the gas station.

"No one saw a silver acrobat," Bradley said in front of the bookstore.

"Maybe the acrobat turned himself invisible!" Nate said.

Brian poked Nate. "Maybe I'll turn *you* invisible!" he said.

Bradley noticed Howard standing outside the window of his barbershop. Next to him was a sign that said SPECIAL SUNDAY HOURS 3–5.

"Let's go ask Howard," Bradley said.

The other kids followed Bradley to the barbershop.

"Did you four sell all your tickets?" Howard asked.

"Yes, we did," Brian said. "But we have a problem."

"Tell me," Howard said. "I love to listen to people's problems."

Just then a man wearing a baseball

cap rushed up to Howard. "Got time to cut my hair?" the man asked.

Howard looked through his window at the wall clock. "It's almost five, so it'll have to be a fast one," he said. "Take off your hat."

The man yanked off his cap. His bushy hair was standing up in all directions.

Howard laughed. "You have a bad case of hat hair," he said, "but I'll take care of that. Go inside and have a seat."

The man walked into Howard's shop. Bradley noticed Lucy watching him. He was trying to smooth down his spiky hair.

"Sorry," Howard said to the kids. "I'm all ears!"

The kids explained about the circus and the acrobat who had vanished.

"We don't know who it is," Nate said. "But all the people who bought tickets would love the act!"

"Gee, I wish I could help," Howard said. "Say, maybe I can! My wife is a great face painter. I'll ask if she wants to join in." Then he rushed into his barbershop to his customer.

"I just had an idea!" Brian said. "Ellie said she'd make popcorn. Howard's wife can paint faces. Maybe we can get other people in town to do stuff for the circus. Maybe we don't even need to find the masked acrobat!"

"Or maybe we've already found her," Bradley said. He turned to Lucy. "You know who it is, don't you?"

Lucy grinned.

7
Meet Pete

Nate and Brian stared.

"You do? Who is it?" Nate asked.

Bradley looked through Howard's window at the clock. "We have to go!" he said. "If we don't get home and eat dinner, we won't be able to go back and see the rehearsal!"

The kids hurried up Main Street. They took Silver Circle to Woody Street, where both Nate and Lucy lived. They stopped in front of Nate's house.

"Let's meet here at ten to seven," Bradley said.

"But you didn't tell us who the acrobat is!" Nate said.

"We'll tell you then!" Bradley said. "Come on, Brian. I'll race you home!"

The twins dashed through Nate's yard and ran to their house on Farm Lane.

An hour and a half later, Bradley, Brian, and Lucy were standing in front of Nate's house. Nate burst through his front door, eating a cookie.

He carried more cookies in a paper napkin.

"Are you planning to share?" Brian asked, eyeing the cookies.

"Duh, that's why I brought three," Nate said. "One for each of you. Ruth Rose and I made them, but they're good anyway."

"Thanks, Nate, you're great!" Lucy said.

"I know I am," Nate said. "Okay, you two, spill the beans. Tell us who you think the acrobat is."

"Let's get going," Bradley said. "I'll tell you on the way."

The kids walked and munched.

"Remember that guy who asked Howard for a haircut?" Bradley asked as they reached the high school grounds.

"Yeah, he had serious hat hair!" Nate said.

"Right," Bradley said. "His hair reminded me—"

Bradley stopped when he saw Adam and Hannah sitting on the bus's bumper. It looked as if something was wrong.

"Hi," Lucy said.

"Hi yourself," Hannah said. She wiped some tears off her cheeks. Then she smiled. "We're the crying Fortunatos today."

Adam giggled. "Better than the dying

Fortunatos," he said. Both teenagers laughed.

"Um, what's going on?" Brian asked.

"Should we tell them?" Adam asked his sister.

"Sure, why not?" she said, wiping her eyes on her sleeve. "They sold tickets for us."

Adam stood up and opened the

sliding door of the bus. "Come on in," he said.

The kids climbed inside the bus and looked around the cozy apartment. There was a bed, a small table with a lamp on it, and a rug on the floor.

In one corner, an old gray parrot sat on a perch. He tilted his head and stared at the newcomers with his shiny black

eyes. "Peter the parrot!" he croaked.

Bradley laughed. "Does he say anything else?" he asked.

Adam scratched the parrot's chest with his finger. "He used to, but now it's just those three words," he said. "We've tried to teach him more, but he pretends he doesn't hear us. Right, Pete?"

"Peter the parrot!" Peter squawked.

Bradley noticed that every inch of wall space held a painting or drawing. Some of them showed circus stuff, like clowns and lions and elephants doing tricks. Bradley realized that the picture he'd found in the shoe box was done by the same artist. He looked at the signature on the bottom of each picture: *Adam.*

One whole wall held pictures of a trapeze artist. An acrobat in silver tights was flying through the air, or swinging from a trapeze bar, or doing flips. Like

the others, these pictures were signed by Adam.

Lucy put her finger on the figure wearing the silver costume. "This is you, right?" she asked Hannah.

8
Lucy's Idea

Hannah blushed. "How did you know?" she asked.

"We saw you yesterday on the trapeze," Lucy said. "I thought you were wonderful!"

"Why, thank you, Lucy!" Hannah said. "But I was in my costume, so how did you know it was me?"

"That's what I want to know!" Brian said.

Bradley told Hannah and Adam about the man at Howard's Barbershop—the one with the messy hair.

"It reminded me of Hannah's the first time we saw her," he said. "That was, like, five minutes after we watched the mystery acrobat in the tent."

"I remember!" Nate said. "Hannah's hair was all spiky."

"After I saw that guy at Howard's, I thought maybe Hannah's hair was all weird because she'd just pulled off that hood on her silver costume!" Bradley went on. "Later, her hair was all neat."

"Our folks don't know," Adam said. "We haven't told them how good Hannah is on the high wire and trapeze."

"But why not?" Bradley asked. "She's awesome!"

Adam sighed. "The folks want to keep the Flying Fortunatos together, but the circus is falling apart," he said. "They're getting old, and they have no money."

"Even if I performed, we still wouldn't have a circus," Hannah said. She looked at her brother. "Tell them the rest, Adam."

"I don't want to be an acrobat anymore," Adam said. "I want to be an artist. I want to go to art school this fall."

"But your parents—" Bradley started to say.

"They don't know that, either," Adam said. "They're going to be crushed when we tell them."

Bradley remembered the note. "Who's Mr. Wood?" he asked Adam.

"How'd you hear about *him*?" Adam asked.

Bradley told him about the picture he'd found in the shoe box. "You wrote the note, right?"

Adam nodded. "Lawson Wood is a great artist," he explained. "I want to do what he does. I was writing him a letter, and then I threw it away."

Adam looked at his sister. "Your turn," he said.

"I don't want to be an acrobat,

either," Hannah said. "I want to open a school to *teach* acrobatics. But the folks would have a fit. They keep thinking they can save the circus."

"She's a natural," Adam said. "She could totally teach other people. I think she's part bird or something."

Hannah grinned. "You're the one who's part bird," she said. Turning to the kids, she added, "Adam Fortunato is the best acrobat I've ever seen. Our parents taught him. Now he's even better than they were. He's been teaching me for ten years!"

Bradley remembered Adam's performance earlier. "Um, we saw you in the tent," he said. "You didn't look much like an acrobat. . . ."

"Oh, I was just practicing how I was going to fool my parents," Adam said. "I was going to pretend I was a klutz— that I couldn't do it anymore. So they'd let me out of the show."

"What are you guys going to do?" Nate asked.

Adam shrugged. Hannah shook her head.

"I have an idea," Lucy said.

Adam and Hannah looked at Lucy. "Tell us!" Hannah said.

"Tell your parents they can be part of the audience tomorrow night," Lucy said.

9
I Can Fly!

"I'm so excited, I can hardly eat my hot dog!" Nate said.

"What do you mean?" Brian asked. "You've already gobbled down two!"

The kids were sitting next to Mr. and Mrs. Fortunato. The couple looked around the crowd with amazement on their faces.

It was intermission time, and in a few minutes, the trapeze act would begin. Every seat in the big tent was taken! Bradley, Brian, Nate, and Lucy were squished between the Fortunatos and Howard the barber.

When Bradley turned around, he saw Mr. Linkletter sitting with three boys who looked like miniature Mr. Linkletters. Bradley waved, and Mr. Linkletter's mustache wrinkled.

Ellie was selling ice cream and hot dogs.

Mr. Paskey, from the Book Nook, stood next to her, handing out bags of hot popcorn.

A band from the high school was playing rock and roll and circus tunes outside the tent.

Inside, a sign stood in front of the trapeze net. But no one could see what it said—it was covered with shiny silver-and-blue fabric.

So far, the audience had seen a man from the senior center juggling fruit, and Officer Fallon doing magic tricks.

Clumsy the clown, who was really Hannah Fortunato, had everybody laughing every time she tripped over her enormous feet.

Now it was almost time for the mystery acrobat. Bradley smiled as the lights went down. The Fortunatos had no idea what they were about to see!

The music ended. A spotlight appeared in the big ring. Everybody cheered when Mr. Holly from the gas station stepped into the circle of light, wearing a bright red jacket and black pants. He held a microphone, and a gold whistle hung around his neck. Peter the parrot sat on his shoulder.

"Good evening, folks," Mr. Holly said. "May I present the world's smartest parrot!" He looked at the bird. "Tell everyone your name, please."

"Peter the parrot!" Peter squawked.

Everyone cheered and whistled.

"Very good, Peter! Now tell everyone the name of the president of the United States," Mr. Holly said.

"Peter the parrot!"

"And who is the vice president, Peter?" Mr. Holly asked.

"Peter the parrot!"

"Very nice, Peter," Mr. Holly said. "Now tell our friends, who is your favorite singer?"

"Peter the parrot!"

"Oh, good! Will you sing a song for us?" Mr. Holly asked.

Peter didn't say anything. He just tucked his head under one wing.

The audience clapped and whistled.

"Now for our special surprise," Mr. Holly said.

"Surprise?" Bradley heard Maude Fortunato ask her husband.

Mr. Holly looked up into the audience, right at Mr. and Mrs. Fortunato. "This next act is dedicated to the Fortunatos by their son, Adam, and their daughter, Hannah!"

The spotlight shone on the high wire.

Maude Fortunato gasped when she saw the figure in silver tights and a mask, balancing on the wire.

"When did Adam get a new costume?" Maude asked her husband. "I just made him the blue one last month!"

"Shhh," her husband said.

Bradley smiled. It was Hannah, not Adam, on the high wire, and she looked great. Only her nose and mouth showed beneath her mask.

The silver acrobat walked across the wire, perfectly balanced. The spotlight followed her. When Hannah reached the other side, she tied a blindfold around her eyes. Then she walked back onto the wire. In the center of the wire, she flipped upside down into a handstand.

The four kids said, "Oooh!" Then they started clapping and whistling.

Maude whispered, "I can't look! Adam has never done this before!"

Hannah flipped again and was on her feet.

Suddenly another acrobat walked to the middle of the wire. This one was dressed in a shiny dark-blue costume and also wore a mask.

The two acrobats joined hands.

"That's Adam!" Maude said. "I made that costume for him. But who's the other one?"

"I think I know," her husband said.

Adam bent one leg, and Hannah stepped onto his knee, still holding his hand. Then she gripped his shoulders and flipped upside down. Before anyone could blink, Hannah's head was balancing on top of Adam's. His arms were raised, and Hannah held both of his hands.

Then, in a flash, Hannah flipped down to the wire. Adam unhitched the trapeze and held it as Hannah climbed onto the bar. Adam pushed the trapeze, and Hannah floated out above the audience.

For the next five minutes, it seemed as if the entire audience was holding its breath. Hannah dipped, soared, flipped, and swung like a silver bird.

Bradley snuck a look at Hannah's

parents. They had tears in their eyes.

When Adam and Hannah flipped down into the net, then onto the ground, everyone jumped to their feet to clap and yell.

Mr. Holly came out and blew his whistle. When the audience quieted down, he handed the microphone to Adam.

Adam and Hannah pulled off their masks.

"Hi, Mom and Dad," Adam said, smiling up at his parents. "So now you know who the real Flying Fortunato is, right?"

Everyone cheered.

"But Hannah has another surprise for you," Adam went on.

The twins each took a corner of the fabric over the sign, then ripped it off.

There on the sign was Adam's most stunning painting yet. It showed Hannah in her silver costume, swinging on the trapeze. The words read:

THE FLYING FORTUNATOS'
SCHOOL OF ACROBATICS

Adam handed the mike to his sister.

"I'll need to hire some teachers," Hannah said. "I hope my first two teachers will be Basilio and Maude Fortunato!"

Her father stood up. "We would be honored, darling!"

"And, Adam!" Maude exclaimed. "Your painting is just as amazing as your performance!"

"Well," Adam began, "about that . . ."

"Hurry up, you slowpokes!" Brian said. "We can't be late for our first class with Hannah!"

The four kids ran toward the tent.

Inside, Bradley, Brian, Nate, and Lucy saw a lot of their school friends. Every kid was wearing a T-shirt with a picture of Hannah in her silver costume. Beneath the picture were the words I CAN FLY!

Basilio handed the kids their new shirts. They pulled them on over the shirts they were wearing.

"Okay, everyone have a seat on the bleachers!" Hannah called out.

The kids all took seats.

Bradley felt a flutter in his stomach. Was he really going to learn how to walk on the high wire or swing on a trapeze?

Adam was there, helping his sister start her school. After counting the kids, he said, "We signed up twenty for this class, but only nineteen are here. Who's missing?"

"That would be me," a deep voice said. They all turned and looked toward the tent's open flap.

Mr. Linkletter walked through. He was wearing high-top sneakers, gym shorts, and a purple T-shirt. "I've always wanted to be a circus performer," he said.

"You can sit next to me, Mr. Linkletter," Bradley said. He scooted over on the bleacher seat.

"Thank you, young Mr. Pinto," Mr. Linkletter said.

Bradley grinned. Mr. Linkletter's mustache was definitely wrinkling!